ISBN 1 85854 582 X
© Brimax Books Ltd, 1997. All rights reserved.
Published by Brimax Books Ltd, Newmarket, England, CB8 7AU, 1997.
Printed in France - n° 70135 - B

Mother Pig's
Big Black
Cooking Pot

BY SUE INMAN

ILLUSTRATED BY ERIC KINCAID

BRIMAX • NEWMARKET • ENGLAND

It was supper time. The three baby pigs came in from the garden where they had been playing. "We're starving!" they said to Mother Pig. "That's good," said Mother Pig. "Supper is almost ready."

"What are you cooking?" asked Peanut Pig. "Something new," said Mother Pig. "Something different, something exciting!"

The three baby pigs looked at each other. They didn't like that idea very much.
"Oh-h-h!" groaned Peanut Pig. "Why can't we have pizza?"
"And apple pie," moaned Parsley Pig.
"With lots and lots of ice-cream!" added Peach Pig.

But it was no good. Mother Pig was hard at work
mixing things in her big, black cooking pot.
"A little of this...
        A little of that...
                Mmmm... Delicious!"

The three baby pigs watched Mother Pig in silence. After a while she placed the pot on the table and handed out three big bowlfuls of steaming stew.
"I don't like this," cried Peanut Pig.
"You haven't even tasted it yet," said Mother Pig.

"It's horrible!" wailed Parsley Pig.
"It's good for you," replied Mother Pig.
"I want pizza!" moaned Peach Pig.
Mother Pig put down her spoon and looked at her children.
"Well in that case, you will have to go to bed without any supper," she said.

So the three baby pigs walked slowly upstairs.
They brushed their teeth and climbed into bed.

They tried to go to sleep. They tried and they tried and they tried.
     But they couldn't.
         They were too hungry.

At last the baby pigs could stand it no longer.
They tiptoed downstairs and crept into the kitchen.
They slowly began to open the fridge door.
They thought of all the apple pie they could eat.

Peanut, Parsley and Peach peered into the fridge.
And what did they find?
NOTHING!
Except for Mother Pig's big, black cooking pot.

"Oh no!" cried the three baby pigs.
"What are we going to do now?" asked Peanut.
"There's only one thing we can do," said Parsley.
"You don't mean...?" said Peach, horrified.
"Yes," said Parsley.

Peanut and Peach watched anxiously while Parsley took a tiny taste of the food in the big, black cooking pot. He closed his eyes and munched thoughtfully.
"It's delicious!" he said at last. "Why don't you both try some?"

Slowly - and carefully - Peanut and Peach *did* try some of the stew. And soon the big, black cooking pot was empty.

Then at last, tired, happy and hungry no more,
the three baby pigs crept back upstairs to bed.
They slept peacefully all night.

In the morning, Mother Pig looked in the fridge.
She was most surprised.
"Well, who could have eaten all that stew?"
she asked herself.

She could not think what had happened to the
left-over stew in her big, black cooking pot.
And no one ever told her.